JURASSIC SENTRIES

ISSUE #4

" DR. KORROSAVE "

Created By
DEION TILLETT

To order additional copies of this book, contact:
Xlibris
844-714-8691
www.Xlibris.com
Orders@Xlibris.com

ISBN: Softcover   978-1-6641-9635-3
        EBook   978-1-6641-9636-0

Print information available on the last page

Rev. date: 10/22/2021

JURASSIC SENTRIES

AQUILLO COMICS

ISSUE #4

" DR. KORROSAVE "

PREVIOUSLY ON

JURASSIC SENTRIES

When the Mayor agrees to let the Sentries live in the city in order to protect the civilians from the Conquers, Rex and the team steak out the city for any sign of their rivals.

During one night on the Sentries potrol, Ankylo ambushes them for making him feel like a failure in their last encounter. While the Sentries are able to hold their own against Ankylo, they were stunned when he uses his club tail to break Rex's leg.

After the Sentries escape safety back to their HQ, Spinus bans Ankylo from persuing the Sentries unless he is ordered to do so and puts Troodon in charge of dealing with them next.

Two days have past now, but something else lurks in the city...

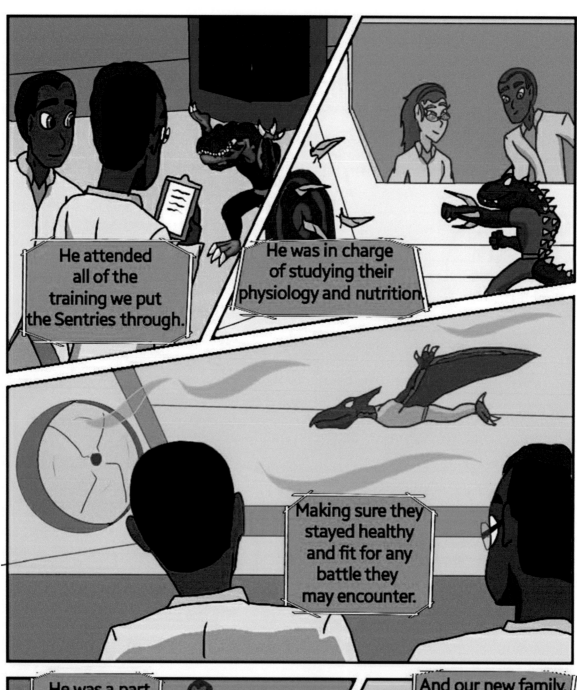
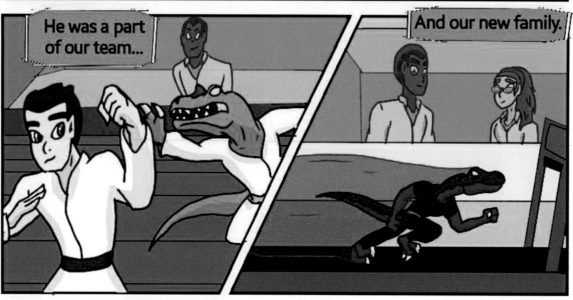

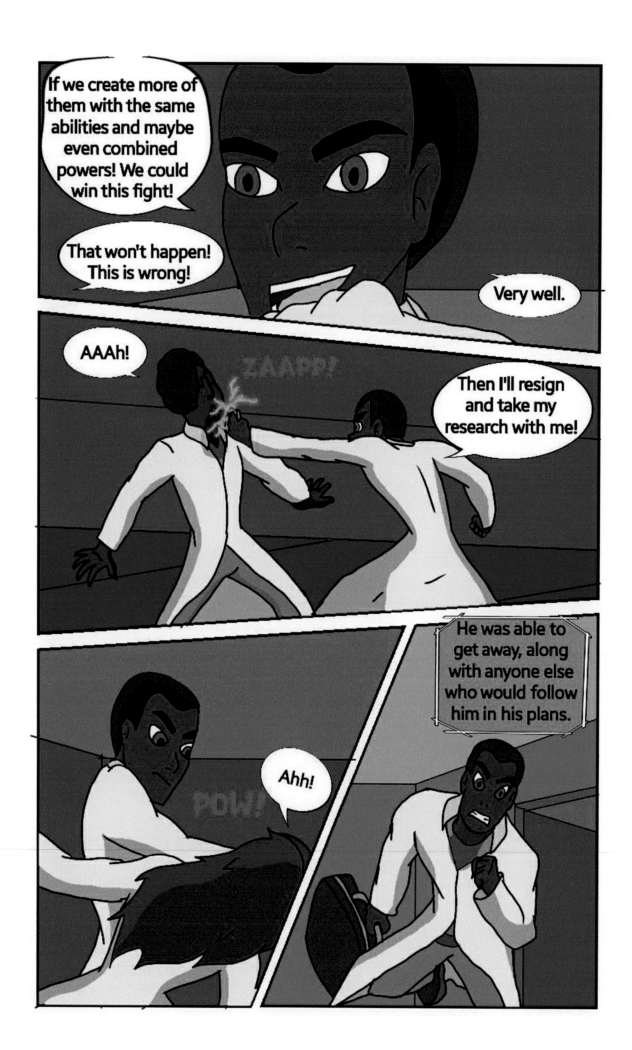

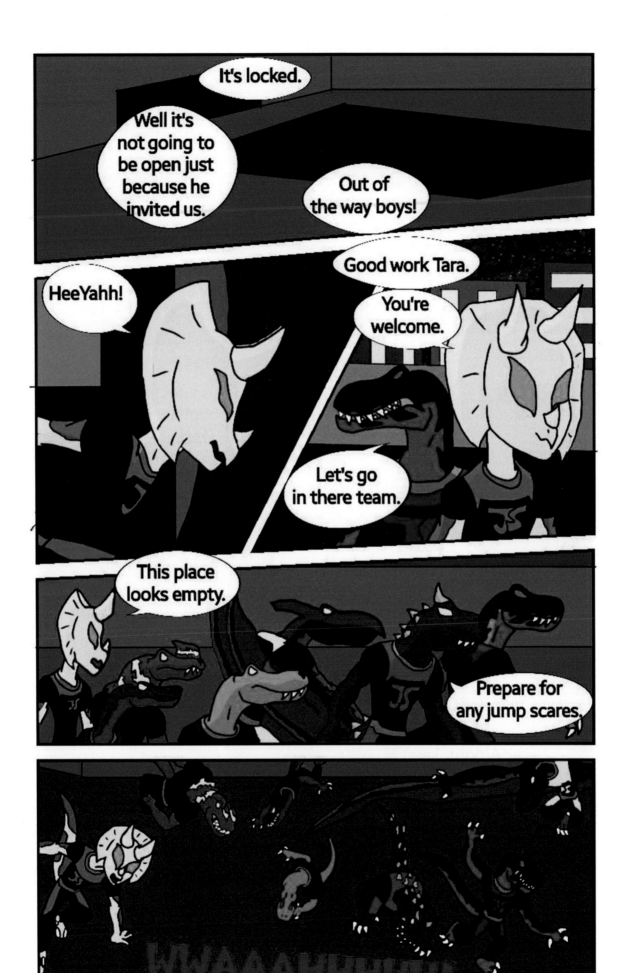

End

JURASSIC SENTRIES

ISSUE #5

NEXT ISSUE : " MUTATIONS "

Created By
DEION TILLETT

Printed in the United States
by Baker & Taylor Publisher Services